D1353172

Look out for other BUTTERFLY MEADOW books:

Dazzle's First Day

Twinkle Dives In

Mallow's Top Team

Skipper to the Rescue

Dazzle's Prickly Problem

Butterfly Meadow

Twinkle and the Busy Bee

Olivia Moss

Illustrated by Sam Chaffey

SCHOLASTIC

With special thanks to Sue Mongredien

First published in the UK in 2008 by Scholastic Children's Books
An imprint of Scholastic Ltd
Euston House, 24 Eversholt Street
London, NW1 1DB, UK
Registered office: Westfield Road, Southam, Warwickshire, CV47 0RA
SCHOLASTIC and associated logos are trademarks and/
or registered trademarks of Scholastic Inc.
Series created by Working Partners Ltd.

ISBN 978 1 407 10659 5

Printed by
CPI Bookmarque, Croydon, CR0 4TD
Papers used by Scholastic Children's Books are made
from wood grown in sustainable forests.

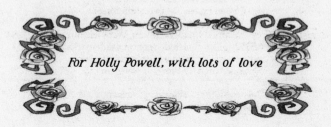

For Holly Powell, with lots of love

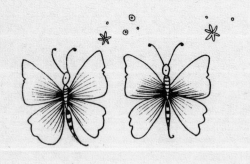

CONTENTS

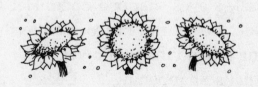

CHAPTER ONE

Mystery in the Meadow

Dazzle was snoozing. It was a hot, sunny afternoon in Butterfly Meadow and she had found a comfortable spot on a sunflower with Skipper and Mallow, two of her butterfly friends. Dazzle was just drifting into a dream about delicious nectar when. . .

"Hey, you guys! There's something wrong in the meadow."

Dazzle's eyes snapped open. Her friend Twinkle, a colourful Peacock butterfly, was zipping around the sunflower.

"What's happening?" Dazzle asked. Twinkle was whizzing about so fast, it made Dazzle's head spin.

Mallow fluttered her small white wings. "Is it a mystery?" she asked, flitting into the air. "I love a good mystery!"

Skipper yawned. "Everything looks fine to me," she said, gazing around. "Twinkle, aren't you hot, racing about?"

Twinkle didn't answer. Instead, she zoomed around the sunflower one more time, her bright colours blurring together as she flew.

"Well?" Dazzle asked. "Aren't you going to tell us what's happening?"

"I'll show you," Twinkle replied mysteriously. "Follow me!"

Dazzle gave her wings a wriggle and fluttered towards her friend with Mallow close behind. "Hey, come on, Skipper," Mallow called back to the Holly Blue butterfly. "It's not like you to miss out on an adventure."

"OK, I'm coming," Skipper said, flapping her pretty blue wings. "Wait for me!"

Twinkle led the butterflies to a thick hedge at the edge of the meadow. She glanced back at the others, then dived down among the leaves. "In here," she instructed.

Dazzle, Skipper and Mallow followed Twinkle, dodging branches. It was cooler out of the sun's glare, but there were thorns on some of the branches, so Dazzle fluttered her pale-yellow wings carefully.

Just then, Twinkle stopped – so suddenly that Dazzle bumped right into her. Then Skipper skidded into the back of Dazzle and

Mallow almost fell out of the hedge, trying to stop in time.

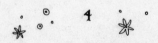

"Whoa!" Mallow yelped, fluttering her wings to steady herself. "Pile-up!"

Dazzle, Twinkle and Skipper untangled themselves, giggling.

"What are we doing in here?" Skipper asked, smoothing her crumpled antennae.

"I'm just about to show you," Twinkle replied. Then she pointed a wing-tip through the hedge to where a cluster of flowers were swaying in the grass below. "There," she said. "See?"

CHAPTER TWO

Help!

Dazzle peered through the leaves but she didn't notice anything unusual. The meadow grass was long and filled with wild poppies, dandelions and cornflowers. "What are we looking at?" she whispered.

"I'm not sure," Mallow said. "Twinkle, what is this? A guessing game?"

"Just wait," Twinkle told them. "Keep watching."

A grasshopper leaped into the butterflies' hiding place, almost landing right on top of

Skipper. "Hey!" she squealed, folding her wings out of his way.

The grasshopper bent his green head low. "I'm sorry," he said, embarassed. "I wasn't expecting to bump into any butterflies in here." "We're solving a mystery," Mallow told him. Twinkle was still gazing out at the flowers. "Look – there it goes again," she said. "*Now* do you see?"

They all stared, even the grasshopper. One of the flowers was vibrating.

"That's only the wind," the grasshopper told them with a laugh. "Now, if you'll excuse me, I'd better hop along." With a huge spring of his back legs, he leaped away and vanished.

"There *is* no wind today," Twinkle said, thoughtfully. "There's something happening in that flower."

Dazzle and her friends slowly made their way through the hedge, until they were level with the flower. They all watched as the blue petals began to shake violently. Dazzle stared. Was something wrong with the flower?

Then there was a faint buzzing, and the flower shook again. Something was inside it! Dazzle glimpsed a small furry body with wings as an insect tumbled out of the flower and plunged to the ground.

Dazzle hid behind Skipper. "What was that?" she whispered.

"I don't know," Skipper replied, leaning out of the hedge for a better look.

"Well, there's only one way to find out," Twinkle decided. "We need to investigate. Come on!"

Dazzle, Twinkle, Skipper and Mallow flew out of the hedge and hovered above the flowers. Dazzle stayed close to her friends. Who knew what the creature might be?

The grass rustled . . . and the butterflies heard a faint moaning. "Help me!" came a scared little voice. "Help!"

CHAPTER THREE

Clueless

Rolling around in the grass was a small insect with black and yellow furry stripes, black legs and two pairs of filmy wings.

"It's a bee!" Dazzle said in surprise. "Hello there."

The bee waved her short front legs when she saw Dazzle. "I'm Sting," she said. "Please, will you help me?"

Dazzle was just about to land beside Sting when Twinkle swooped down next to her. "Be careful," she whispered. "You know what bees are like. They have sharp stingers. She could hurt you!"

Dazzle looked at Sting, struggling, in the grass. She knew that bees had stingers, but she couldn't ignore an insect asking for help. She dodged Twinkle and flew down to the little bee. "What's wrong?" she asked. "Are you hurt?"

"No," Sting replied. "But I'm lost. It's my first time out gathering pollen for my hive and I've worked hard all day. Look!" She held up her back legs, and Dazzle could see that the fine hairs on them were full of pollen. "Now I'm tired and want to go home," the bee went on, "but I can't remember the way back to my hive and I'm loaded down with all this pollen."

"We'll help you," Skipper said kindly, hovering near Dazzle. "Come on, fly up with us. I'm sure together we can get you home."

Sting's face lit up and she tried to launch herself into the air – but she was carrying so much pollen, she could only fly for a few seconds before plummeting back down to the grass.

"I'm so tired," she explained. "I don't know if I can fly any more."

"Oh dear," Twinkle said. "Tell you what, I'll whizz around the meadow and see if I can spot any other bees. They'll be able to tell us the way to your hive. They might even be able to help you get back there." She shook her large wings with a flourish. "I'm Twinkle, by the way, and these are my friends; Skipper, Dazzle and Mallow," she said.

Sting waved a leg shyly. "Hi," she said. "Thank you for helping me."

"Here, Sting," Mallow said, landing on a nearby flower. The head of the flower dipped towards the bee. "Have some nectar while we wait for Twinkle to come back. It might give you a bit more energy."

Sting smiled and sipped the nectar gratefully with her long tongue, while Skipper and Dazzle used her wings to fan her. Dazzle exchanged an anxious glance with Skipper. She really hoped they could help the little bee get home.

A few moments later, Twinkle returned. "Sorry, Sting," she said, floating down to land. "I looked everywhere in the meadow. No bees. I asked a couple of wasps and a gang of flies, but they don't know of any beehives around here. They hadn't seen your friends either. It looks like they all went back to the hive without you."

Sting's smile faded. "I don't know what to do," she said, tears welling in her eyes. "How will I get home now?"

Dazzle grabbed some soft, springy moss to dry Sting's tears. "Hey, it's OK," she said softly. "We'll help you get home. All you need to do is think hard about which way you flew into the meadow. Then we'll just go back that way."

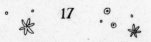

"That's the problem," Sting said. "I was so busy collecting pollen, I didn't watch where I was going. All I know is that I live in a hollow tree covered with honeysuckle . . . but I don't have a clue how to get back there!"

CHAPTER FOUR

Into the Blue

"Once you've had a rest, you might remember *something* if we all fly together," Skipper suggested. "It won't seem so bad when you're not alone."

Mallow wiggled her antennae, then launched into a cheer:

"S–T–I–N–G.

We will find that hollow tree!

One, two, three, four, five.

Butterflies heading to the hive!"

Sting smiled at Mallow's rhyme. "I do feel a bit better," she said. "Thanks.

That was great. Let's try flying together."

She buzzed slowly into the air, trying hard to fly, even though she was weighed down. The butterflies fluttered up to join her and they set off around the meadow. "Does anything look familiar?" Dazzle asked hopefully as they passed a patch of golden buttercups. Sting gazed around, then shook her head. "Not really," she said. "But let's keep going. I don't want to give up yet!"

They flew on a bit further. "Do you recognize this big old tree?" Skipper asked, pointing it out with her wing.

"Well, yes. . ." Sting started. She landed on a branch and looked around; then her wings slumped. "Oh, I'm all mixed up!" she exclaimed. "And I've got to get all my pollen home – I was really hoping the queen bee would be proud of me for collecting so much."

"There must be a way we can help our new friend," Twinkle muttered. She fanned her wings, making them sparkle in the sunshine.

Dazzle and Skipper couldn't help but stare. "All those beautiful colours," Skipper murmured and Twinkle smiled.

"That's it!" she said, "I always remember the lovely colours I see along the way when I go somewhere new. Sting, all you have to do is think about what colours you spotted on your way here. Then you can find your way home."

"Oh, good idea, Twinkle!" Skipper said at once. "I always notice blue flowers, especially if they're the same shade as my wings."

"I like yellow best," Dazzle said, fluttering her pale-yellow wings proudly.

"Close your eyes and think, Sting," Mallow urged. "Before you reached the meadow, what's the last colour you remember seeing?"

Sting closed her eyes and was silent for a moment. Then her wings shook with excitement. "It's working!" she said. "I can remember seeing blue below me as I flew – blue, everywhere!"

Twinkle did a loop-the-loop. "I know exactly where Sting means!" she cried. "Cornflower Valley. Follow me!" And with a flash of her bright wings, she zoomed up and away.

CHAPTER FIVE

The Trail Begins...

Dazzle, Skipper, Mallow and Sting followed Twinkle. Sting was flying much faster now as they journeyed across the meadow and all the way up Juniper Hill.

Twinkle paused, bobbing up and down excitedly. "Look! Look!" she cried to the others as they approached. "There's blue *everywhere* down there."

Dazzle gazed down into the valley. Of course! Below them stretched a carpet of blue cornflowers.

Sting buzzed with delight. "Yes – this is it," she cried, beaming. "I was definitely here before. I remember!"

Twinkle smiled. "I *thought* you might be

talking about Cornflower Valley," she said
happily. "It's one of my favourite places.
So now we know you came into Butterfly
Meadow from this direction."

But Sting didn't seem to be paying attention. She was too busy gazing at all the beautiful cornflowers. "So many flowers, so much pollen to collect," she buzzed to herself. Before the butterflies could stop her, she went whizzing off towards the blooms.

"Sting! Sting!" called Twinkle, flying after her. "Stop – wait! You can't start collecting more pollen now."

"But I must," Sting replied, zooming down to the first clump of cornflowers. "I've got to get as much pollen as I can. I want the queen bee to see that I'm a good worker."

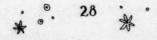

"You *are* a good worker, Sting, I'm sure the queen bee knows that," Dazzle told her. "But if you collect any more pollen, it will make you even heavier!"

"The sun will be setting soon," Mallow reminded the little bee. "We have get you home before it's dark. Once the sun goes down, the colours will be harder to see."

Sting backed away from the cornflowers. "You're right," she said. "I just don't want to disappoint the queen bee. She's very grand, you know."

"Yes, we know," Skipper said. "We met her at Sports Day."

"She gave us each a touch of golden pollen on our wings," Mallow remembered, wriggling happily at the thought.

Twinkle clapped her wings together. "We need to keep moving," she reminded them all.

"Now, Sting. You did well to remember the cornflowers. But what colours can you remember seeing before you got here to the valley?"

Sting thought about it for a moment. "I remember a circle of green," she said slowly. "With white dots on it."

Dazzle felt puzzled. She had no idea where this could be – she had never seen white dots on green anywhere! "Daisies in a field?" she guessed.

Sting shook her head. "I don't think so," she said. "The dots were bigger than daisies."

"Oh dear," Twinkle said when nobody could come up with any other ideas. "Doesn't anybody know where this place could be? Surely the trail hasn't gone cold already?"

If we can't solve this riddle, Dazzle thought. *We may never find Sting's home.*

CHAPTER SIX

Wake Up, Sting!

Suddenly Mallow zipped
high in the air, her antennae
quivering. "Got it!" she
exclaimed, whizzing
back down to the others
again. "Sting, were the
white dots near water?"
she asked.

"Yes," said Sting.
"Lots of water."

Mallow laughed.
"The dots are water

lilies," she explained to her butterfly friends. "And the green must be all the lily pads. I think she's talking about Cowslip Pond."

All the butterflies knew where that was. They had flown a relay race around Cowslip Pond during Sports Day. The pond's cool water was always refreshing on a hot summer's day.

"This way, Sting," Dazzle said, fluttering into the air once more.

Off they all went, Dazzle in front, leading the colourful procession through Cornflower Valley and on towards the pond. Once they arrived at the cool green water, the butterflies and Sting all flew to rest in the shade of a large leafy tree nearby.

"Phew," sighed Dazzle. She was hot and tired. Her wings ached and she felt very thirsty. "Where now, Sting? Is it much further?"

Sting let out a yawn. "I don't know," she admitted. "It's been such a long day," she said, "and being a worker bee is such . . . hard . . . work. . ."

Dazzle peered at Sting, wondering why she was talking so slowly. Then a tiny snore drifted through the air and Dazzle saw that her eyes were shut.

"She's fallen asleep," Skipper said. "She must be worn out, poor thing."

"She can't sleep now!" Twinkle cried. "We've got to get her back to the hive before it gets dark."

"We'll have to wake her," Mallow decided. "Sting? Sting! Wakey wakey!"

Sting didn't stir, so Dazzle plucked a

blade of grass and tickled the little bee's nose with it.

"Bzzzzzz. . ." Sting said sleepily, rubbing her nose and rolling over. She was still fast asleep!

Skipper found a sweet-smelling white petal and waved it under Sting's nose. "This yummy smell will wake her up," she said.

Sure enough, Sting sniffed the air . . . but then snorted and carried on snoozing.

"S – T – I – N – G! Wake up, little honeybee!" cheered Mallow – but even that didn't wake her.

The four butterflies looked at one another anxiously. "We've got to wake her and get going again," Dazzle said. "It'll be dark soon, and we won't stand a chance of helping Sting home if we can't see where we're going. But she's sleeping so soundly. What can we do?"

CHAPTER SEVEN

A Friend Helps Out

Twinkle spread her wings wide. "I know who can help us," she called, sounding excited. "I'll be right back!"

39

Dazzle, Skipper and Mallow watched her fly to the top of a tall sturdy tree. "What *is* she doing?" Skipper asked.

Mallow shook her head. "Who knows?" she replied. "Twinkle is always full of surprises."

"She's coming back, look," Dazzle said, spotting her friend's bright wings among the leaves.

"And who's that with her?" Skipper asked, peering into the sunny sky. A creature was flying down with Twinkle. It was much larger than a butterfly, but it was hard to tell what it was with the sun shining in their eyes.

The creature gave a loud "ha-ha-ha!" noise as if it were laughing, and the butterflies all looked at one another in bewilderment.

"It's a bird," Skipper realized, as the creature drew closer. "Oh, isn't it gorgeous? As colourful as a butterfly!"

Dazzle stared at the new arrival. With its emerald-green back feathers, pale-yellow underbelly and crimson head, she had

never seen such a
colourful bird. But why was it
laughing at them?

Twinkle landed next to her
friends, closely followed by the bird,
who bent his head in a polite bow.

"This is Boom – he's a woodpecker,"
Twinkle announced.
"He's just what we
need to wake Sting.
Watch this!"

Boom flew up to
perch on a branch close
to the tree trunk and
started tapping at the
wood very fast with
his beak. *Drrr-rrrr-rrrr!*

41

went his sharp beak as it pecked away at the wood.

Dazzle could hardly think straight with the noise. It was so loud!

Sting's eyes snapped open at once and she looked around wildly. "Oh! Oh! What's happening?" she cried. "Who's knocking?"

Dazzle put out a comforting wing. "It's OK, Sting," she said. "Nobody's knocking – it's just Boom up there, see?"

Boom gazed down, his eyes merry and bright. "Just pecking for grubs," he called to Sting with a friendly wave of one green wing. "Oooh . . . ants. Let me at those ants!" And off he went again. His beak tapped against the wood so quickly, it became a blur.

"Now, Sting," Twinkle said loudly over Boom's pecking, "no falling asleep again. We need to get you home, remember?"

"What's our next colour clue?" Mallow asked. "Can you remember anything else that might help us find the way back to your hive?"

Sting thought for a moment. "All I can remember is my home," she said with a shrug of her gauzy wings. "The hive is in a big, hollow tree which is covered with honeysuckle. The flowers on the honeysuckle just opened the other week – they are creamy white, and they smell delicious."

"Hmmm," Skipper said. "I don't remember seeing that tree."

Dazzle shook her head. "Me neither," she said. "Sorry, Sting."

Boom suddenly gave a cry. "Ha-ha-ha! I know that tree," he told them. "Hollow trees always make the best sound. Your honeysuckle tree isn't far from here. Follow me."

Boom spread his glossy wings and took off into the air.

"What are we waiting for?" Dazzle cried. "Let's go!"

She and her friends fluttered after the woodpecker. Dazzle had to flap her wings hard to keep up – and when she glanced back to check on Sting, she saw that the little bee was lagging behind. "Keep going, Sting," Dazzle urged, waiting for her to catch up.

Boom
led them into
a nearby forest.
As soon as they
had passed a few trees,
Sting suddenly let out a
joyful shout. "Hey! I recognize
this place," she cried. "I'm almost
home!"

CHAPTER EIGHT

Home at Last

Dazzle thought Sting might burst with excitement and happiness! The little bee was buzzing loudly and flying really fast despite her heavy load. A tall tree with a hole in its side loomed up ahead of them. Masses of white flowers bloomed on the climbing honeysuckle plant that rambled all around the trunk and along the tree's branches.

"Thank you, oh, thank you!" Sting said, buzzing around in a circle. "It's so good to be back!"

"My pleasure, little one," Boom said. "Goodbye, everyone. Nice to meet you."

"Goodbye, Boom!" the butterflies and Sting called, waving their antennae at him as he flew away.

"Try the honeysuckle nectar," Sting urged the butterflies, flying to one of the white flowers. "It tastes so good."

The butterflies unrolled their long curled tongues to sip the sweet nectar. "Ahh, that's better," Skipper said after a long drink. "Thank you."

"Let me show you my home," Sting said,

buzzing up to the hive entrance. "If you peep in from here, you won't get honey on your wings. Come and see!"

Dazzle and her friends hovered at the edge of the hive, peering inside. The bees' nest looked waxy, with cells and corridors leading away from the central open space. Two worker bees stood guard at the entrance, and inside, lots of other bees rushed around, carrying nectar and pollen to feed their young.

"Wow!" Mallow exclaimed. "It's so busy in there!"

"I can smell the honey," Dazzle said, breathing in the sweet air.

Sting bobbed up and down, looking proud of her fellow bees. Just then, a large bee came out of one of the chambers and floated over to them. It was the queen bee!

She had thick furry stripes on her body, and the most elegant buzz Dazzle had ever heard.

"There you are, Sting," the queen bee said. "We've been so worried about you.

Where have you been?"

Sting explained what had happened and told the queen bee how the butterflies had helped her find her way home.

"You did a wonderful job collecting so much pollen," the queen bee told her. "But you must be more careful next time – stay with your friends and don't stray too far from the hive."

Sting lowered her antennae and nodded. "Of course," she said humbly.

The queen bee turned to the butterflies. "I'm so grateful to you for helping Sting," she said. "Is there anything I can do to say thank you?"

Twinkle dipped her wings and gave a little curtsy. "Well, I've always wanted to taste honey," she said.

The queen bee smiled. "Then let's get you some!" she said.

One of the worker bees flew over, carrying a sticky blob of honey between her front legs, and gave each butterfly a drop to try.

"Oooh," said Dazzle, enjoying the sticky sweetness. "It's delicious."

"Thank you," Skipper said gratefully. "What a treat!"

The queen bee glanced out of the hollow. "It's getting dark," she said. "Would you like to stay the night here? There's plenty of room."

"That's kind of you," Mallow replied, "but our home is in Butterfly Meadow. If we set off right away and fly fast, we'll be able to make it there by nightfall."

The queen bee nodded. "I understand," she said. "There's no place like home."

"Thanks again," Sting said to her new friends. "And goodbye. See you soon, I hope!"

Dazzle, Mallow, Skipper and Twinkle all waved their wings to say goodbye, before setting off for Butterfly Meadow.

Dazzle felt tired as the four friends fluttered away. "We flew a long way today," she said.

"We did," Mallow agreed. "But we made a new friend *and* tasted some delicious honey, too. All thanks to Twinkle spotting

Sting by the hedge."

Twinkle chuckled. "Being a butterfly sure is a lot of fun!" she said.

"Absolutely," said Skipper. "I wonder what will happen tomorrow?"

Dazzle smiled at the thought. "I can't wait to find out," she said, flying through the sunset sky.

Want to know all about the butterflies
in the meadow?

Dazzle

Pale Clouded Yellow butterfly

Likes: Dancing and making friends

Dislikes: Being left out

Twinkle

Peacock butterfly

Likes: Her beautiful wings

Dislikes: Getting wet!

Mallow

Cabbage White butterfly

Likes: Organizing parties and activities

Dislikes: Being bored

Skipper

Holly Blue butterfly

Likes: Helping others

Dislikes: Birds who try to eat her!

Read about more adventures in
Butterfly Meadow

FLUTTERY, FRIENDLY FUN

Butterfly Meadow

Dazzle's First Day

Olivia Moss

FLUTTERY, FRIENDLY FUN

Butterfly Meadow

Twinkle Dives In

Olivia Moss

FLUTTERY, FRIENDLY FUN

Butterfly Meadow

Mallow's Top Team

Olivia Moss

FLUTTERY, FRIENDLY FUN

Butterfly Meadow

Skipper to the Rescue

Olivia Moss

FLUTTERY, FRIENDLY FUN

Butterfly Meadow

Dazzle's Prickly Problem

Olivia Moss